The Raindrops, you see,
were going back to the sea
where there were no roads to be found.
For this journey began in a pipe underground.

Puddle, Piddle and Diddle
were all crushed into the middle
with a billion other drops there too.
As one big funnel swept them into a tunnel,
it was just like going down the loo.

The Raindrops
Down The Drain

Written and Illustrated By Glenn McLernon

Twirling and whirling and swirling,
the Raindrops went hurtling and durtling,
as the big flood began to wane;
down, down, down
into the dark, cold, slimy drain.

Far beneath the ground,
the old pipe went around,
through the earth and over some rock,
where a shy little earthworm
peeped out from an old buried sock.

With one big gasp, they went like a blast
around one bend and then by another.
"Steady on now." Said Puddle.
"Aye, aye." Said Piddle.
"Oh! I wish I'd been nicer to my mother."

The Raindrops all rushed through the dirty old pipe.
It was dark, as dark as dark as the night.
Then suddenly less dimmer,
a hope and a glimmer :
A tiny little peep of daylight.

With a great big whoosh; they shot over a bush.
They were sailing right through the bright air.
Now at last they were free,
like a wild honey bee,
on their way back down to the sea.

They were bished and bashed and bumped
as they tumbled to a dirty old pond below,
where some uncaring person had dumped
an old bike, a chair
and a big orange pillow.

"Where are we?" Said Puddle. "Oh dear.
Some dirty old pond, I fear."
"It's slimy." Said Diddle.
"And horrible." Said Piddle.
"It's quite clear, we cannot stay here."

They jumped onto a branch of a tree,
that was going their way to the sea.
It floated away down the cold river,
so cold that it made them all shiver.

They were having such fun
as they floated along,
while the river flowed down to the sea.
"Ah! Ah!" Said Puddle.
"And hee, hee." said Diddle.
"This is the life for me."

They floated along beneath the warm sun,
past some thirsty old cows, you see.
"Careful, now." Said Piddle
"And steady," said Diddle,
"or they'll lick us all up for their tea."

A curious dog swam out to their log
and quickly swam back to the shore.
"Well goodness." Said Piddle.
"And gracious." Said Diddle.
"Now that was a bit of a bore."

They went under a bridge.
It was cool as a fridge
and they floated right through like a breeze.
"A.....tishoo". Went Diddle."
"And bless you." Said Piddle.
Well that was a heck of a sneeze.

Diddle kept watch while the others were asleep.
He looked down into the water so deep,
where he could see the little fishes,
all snuggled up, fast asleep.

The river flowed into a lake.
The Raindrops dived down for some fish cake,
when suddenly a wave
pushed them into a cave
where they met an old fish called Dave.

Old Dave had a warning
for the Raindrops that morning....
"Be careful my friends.
I don't wish to offend
but there's danger beyond the next bend."

They snoozed and they doozed as they floated along
and the sun was shining so bright.
"Wake up." Cried Puddle.
"I think we're in trouble.
"Old Dave in the cave; he was right."

The danger was clear to all.
They were heading towards a big waterfall
Piddle said. "Great.
I really can't wait.
It will be just like jumping over a wall."

"Hold on tight." Said Puddle.
"This waterfall will be no trouble.
We're going over the edge
and I give you my pledge,
we'll be safe, as if we're in a bubble."

Fast, then faster and faster to the edge.
Then faster and faster and faster.
They couldn't fight the pull.
They were going like a mad bull
as they went right over the edge.

Poor old Puddle, Piddle and Diddle.
Would they survive at all
or would they get crushed in the fall?

They pulled their rip-cords
and their parachutes opened wide.
"Wowee, hehee, yippee." They all cried.
And down, down, down they did glide.

Together, they landed so well
in a big bumpy, watery swell.
It was cold, it was rough
but they had to be tough
as they drifted away like the sound of a bell.

They bumped into a rock
and got a big shock
as their heads went . . .
tick tock, tick tock, tick tock
just like some old grandfather clock

The waters were bad and the waves were mad.
Then their old branch came by like a boat.
They jumped on with a cry
as the branch drifted by
and away down the rapids they did float.

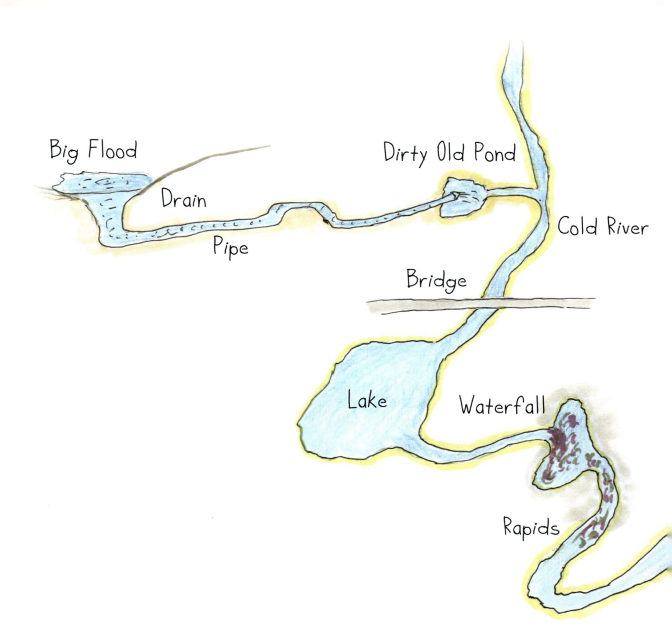

So remember their trip down the river
From the flood, down the drain and through the old pipe.
Remember old Dave
and the grim warning he gave
and the waterfall that made them take flight.

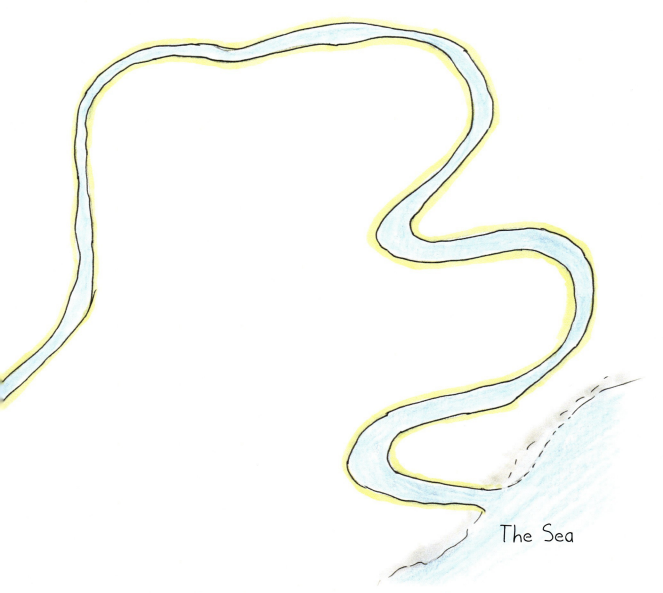

The Sea

So what might happen next?
Will there be another big test?
Where would they go and where would they flow?
Would they swim, would they float or would they just row?

So there you are and there you have it and that's what it's all about.

Watch out for the next rhyming story as
the Raindrops continue their journey to the sea.

Coming soon: The Raindrops: On the River

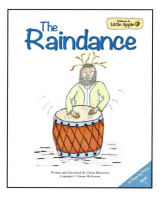 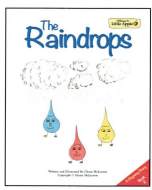 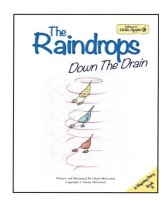 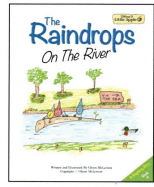

Stories from Little Apple

The Little Apple stories are a collaboration by
Glenn McLernon and Lorraine Harvey

The Raindrops: Down the Drain
First published in 2014 by Glenn McLernon
Phone: 07503184650 (UK)
E.mail: gmclernon@googlemail.com

ISBN: 978-0-9929145-2-3

A catalogue record of this book is available from the British Library.